YOU ARE MY
HOPE

BY

AMY MANNING

Copyright © 2024

AMY MANNING

Ebook ISBN: 978-1-964818-45-0
Paperback ISBN: 978-1-964818-46-7
Hardback ISBN : 978-1-964818-47-4

All Rights Reserved. Any unauthorized reprint or use of this material is strictly prohibited. No part of this book may be reproduced or transmitted in any form or by any means, electronic or mechanical, including photocopying, recording, or by any information storage and retrieval system without express written permission from the author.

All reasonable attempts have been made to verify the accuracy of the information provided in this publication. Nevertheless, the author assumes no responsibility for any errors and/or omissions

DEDICATION

Dedicated to my Family and Friends.

I could not do life without you!

Contents

Author Bio

Amy Manning is from Colorado raised in the Midwest. An outdoor enthusiast, A world traveler, Chef, who loves to work with children, and lead Bible studies.

Differences

Why do we look at others differently?
We only see what we want to see, and we don't take the time to get to know a person.
We judge them before we know them.
Every person has value.
Many times we don't value life as we should; maybe it's because we don't care like we should.
If you see a person that looks differently than you, try and find a way to look past the differences.
The world is full of 7 billion, yet most are lonely.
Life is too short to end your own.
Life is too precious and sweet to take away.
If you can save one more life, it is worth it.
Reach out and be a friend to those who need a friend.
Do you see the value each life makes? God does!
Let us make time to help those in need.
Let's be the listening ear they need.
We all need each other and everyone needs help sometimes.
Next time you see someone being bullied or made fun of, don't join in but rather stand up for them.
Everyone longs to be loved and a have friend to share life with.
Let's be the voice of the voiceless.
May we stand up for the weak and helpless.
After all every person has been made in the image of God.
I believe we live in a colorful world where we can learn to appreciate others who come from different cultures and places then we do. Let's take the time to learn from each other.
My hope is that we can see each other through God's eyes only; then can we increase the value, the beauty of each person.

Onething 2013

Come away my beloved, let me fill you with My Love.
A love that is for the lost, broken, and children.
My love is a lasting love, but other people's love fades away.
Abide in Me and there you will find satisfaction.
Don't give up on Me I will not give up on you.
I will never leave you or forsake you.
Stay in My Word there you will find My will.
Keep a humble and teachable heart.
Stay on the right path.
For My path leads to everlasting life.

Onething 2017

Worship the one who is worthy.
Who/what do you worship?
Worship the One who made you!
You are His child the one in whom He delights in.
Let Jesus be the one you praise.
Shout to the one who is worthy.
Sing a new song to Jesus.
You were created to give God glory!
Let His love shine through you.
After all you bare the image of God.
So, will you give your life to be used for His purpose and glory?

Who will Invest in the Next Generation?

Each generation needs each other.
I need the wisdom of generations that have gone before me.
I can also learn from the age groups that are younger then me.
I'm thankful for the legacy that my great grandparents, grandparents, and parents have left.
What are you doing to invest in the generations younger or older then you?
What can we do to see the gaps of each generation that is alive come together?
When I read the genealogy's in the Bible I see that God is for generations and families and that they are meant to be united as one.
I know that prayer can make a difference in seeing reconciliation between nations, people groups, and generations that are at animosity with each other.
Only God can change a heart to give and receive forgiveness for all the injustice that been shed. It's when we allow God's love to come in that we can make room to forgive those who have used, abused, mistreated, or persecuted us.
Maybe like me you have asked why is there so much injustice and suffering in this world?
I believe because we all have free wills and are born with a sinful nature this is why there is unfairness and wrong deeds committed.
Unfortunately, the next generation has to live with the consequences the generations before them have made whether they want too.
Making restitution is not easy, but a must if we want to grasp harmony and transformation.
Many claim they want to see peace, but they are not even at peace with in themselves. Reconciliation must first start with you, then you can reach your family, neighbors, village, city, state, nation, and world.

The Cross

Jesus what was it like to die on the wood you created?
Did you want to leave your home in heaven when God sent you as a babe to this earth?
Thirty-three years was the time it took for you to fulfill the missions God had for you to do.
You obediently went to the cross even if you wished for another way.
You willing took my punishments, so I could be saved from my sins.
Thank you, Jesus, for sheading Your blood for me, so I could be set free.
You made a way for everyone who calls on the name of the Lord to be forgiven of their sins.
It is finished, the work has been done, and now I can spend eternity in heaven with Jesus.

Love wins

Love wins every time you choose to love
Love is not a feeling, but choice you make
Time is one way to spell love
Love wins every time you forgive and every time you serve
others
Love wins when you are patient, kind, not jealous, proud, or
boastful
Love never gives up hope, but keeps on even when you want to
quite and give up on hope
Love is greater than faith and hope
Love last the longest
It's His love that that draws us to Him
There is a time and purpose for everything
A time for love and hate
A time for life and death
A time to plant and harvest
A time to kill and a time to heal
A time to build up and tear down
A time to laugh and a time to greave
A time to embrace and not to embrace
A time for war and peace
A time to speak and a time not to talk
Love is stronger than death
Love is like the brightest fire quenching all fear
You cannot buy love
The waters can't quench love
Love walks with you though the fire and trials of life.
It is there when you feel like you can't go on with life
Love holds you when the tears can't stop.
Love quenches all fears, sadness, and tears.
After all love wins!

Ecc 3:1-8
1Cor. 13

Love

When I think about love I think of a parent and child and the love that bonds them together.
When I think about love I think about a wedding and the couple choosing to spend the rest of their life together.
When I think about love I think of a savior who shed His blood for me.
When I think about love I think of how I'm made to need love and give love away!
When I think about love I think of a friend that will lay his/her life down for another.
That is love to me.

Hope

I can see a child in pain, a child that wants someone to love him.
I believe everyone wants to be loved. As the years go by the
child wonders what is wrong with me. Why am I not worthy of
love? Can't you see the hopelessness. Can't you see the fear.
Can't you see I need someone to let me I have value.
We are all made in the image of God, but not everyone knows
this. So, we fill the emptiness with things that will never satisfy
us. If only everyone had someone that believed their life
mattered, and spoke life into them instead of death.
You should use your words to bring life not harm. Let those
around you know they are worth loving. Life should be valued,
but all too often we don't value it as we should. We stand by
while others are in pain. We think we cannot make a difference
with all lives, so we do nothing for the ones we can. Use your
lifespan to bring hope, life, and God's love to those who need it
the most. After all every life is worth so much to God. If we all
did our part to love the hurting and unwanted the world would be
a much richer place.

Life, Keep Fighting

We've had out up and downs, but I could not imagine you not being here.
So please fight for your life.
Don't you see how valuable your life is?
Think before you act, and know that I'm just a call away!
If you are having a hard day run to Jesus.
You can always ask me for prayer.
I get that life is not easy, and that life doesn't always go the way we think is should.
That's why we've got to keep pressing on knowing that there is so much in store for us when we reach heaven.
So, keep fighting and know that I'm on your side praying for you.

Heaven

What comes to my mind when I think of heaven?
All my fears, tears, and pain will be gone.
What will I want to do when I first arrive?
Will I see my loved ones?
I can't wait to give Jesus a hug.
Heaven is a place where there is love, joy, and peace.
Heaven is forever and my mind cannot comprehend this!
All the colors, sights, and sounds.
I imagine I will hear worship, water running, voices talking.
I see smiles and hear laughter because there is no sadness in heaven.
I can walk on the streets of gold.
I wonder what I will eat at the love feast in heaven?
The love is thick there.
The joy is all-around me.
The peace is so real I can feel it.
Why would I not want to go to heaven where Jesus is preparing a place for me if only, I believe in Him.
Heaven is worth more than money can buy or the biggest diamond ring I can find.
Heaven is my home this earth will pass away, but heaven is eternal.
So I will keep my eyes on the eternal things.

Saying Goodbye

As one life ends a new life begins.
Our days are numbered.
Only God knows when we will breathe our first breath and take our final breath.
When we know Jesus there is no fear in death.
As hard as it is to say goodbye to those we love, there is hope when we know we will see them again.
It is more of a see you later than goodbye.
Oh, what a reunion when we will see the ones, we love that have gone before us.
The place the Lord has prepared for us is a place of no pain, no crying, no shame, no hurt, and no sin.
Heaven is a place of joy, love, and worship.
So, cherish the time you have left with your loved ones.
Make the most of the days you have on earth.
Live without fear knowing God has your life in His hands.

Transparent with Others

This generation is crying out for someone to be real with them.
They can see the right though the phoniness of man.
So, what is stopping you from being real.
Are you afraid of what others may see?
Are you troubled by what you see in the mirror each day?
Open up let them see the real you not the fake you, but who you really are in Christ.

The Artist

I see an Artist each time I see a sunrise or sunset.
As I look around, I see so many faces and places I see that they
did not just happen out of happenstance.
When I look at the majestic mountains, the never-ending ocean,
the wild flowers, the prairies, and the hot desert I know there
must be a Creator.
I know the Designer who created all of this.
He is real.
He wants to have a relationship with you.
He made you unique there is not another person like you.
So, don't compare yourself to others.
After all He loves you just the way you are.
When I look in the mirror I see a Designer that can only make
beautiful things.
Just look at our bodies and the way they were formed and the
way they function this is how I know I have an awesome
Creator.
Only God can do all of this.
Creator, Designer, Maker, and Artist that is who He is to me.
Who is God to you?
How do you see the God who made you?

The Wonder of God

When I see the mountains, I realize how BIG God is.
As I look at the people all around me, I see God is very detail oriented.
When I gaze at the ocean, I know that God has big plans for me, so much more than I can imagine.
Take a look at the tallest tree and, oh, how I feel so small.
I see the beauty of God in the wild flowers that grow in the spring.
I see His love as the waves crash the shore line.
When I look at the vast stars at night, I see He knows all their names.
I realize the way He provides for the animals and how much more will He provided for you and me.
God is so much more awesome then I have ever imagined!
He is the best thing that has ever happened to me.
Take a look around. What do you see?
I see a God of compassion.
I understand He can count all the hair on my head.
I see a heavenly Father that knows me so much better than my earthly family ever will.
Look at the sunrise and sunset, and see what an artist He is.
I see that I have hands to bless, serve, and touch others' lives.
I have eyes to see others the way He sees them.
I have ears to hear His voice and listen to others as they tell their stories.
I have a voice to stand up for all the injustice I see. I have a mouth to tell of the love of Jesus.
I have feet to travel the world.
So, what do you have? How can Jesus use you?
I want to be one to say "Yes" to the call of God.
Will you be His hands and feet?
I love how the creation all around me tells of a Creator.
I want to meditate on the goodness of God.
I want to remain thankful.
God rejoices when one life turns to Him.

Each day is a new day to love and serve Jesus, who bled and died for you and I.
Let me sing His praises, in the morning, noon, and night.
Lord, help us all use our gifts to bring you glory.
Share your story, and let God use you to go on some wild and amazing journeys with Him.
So, as I think of the wonder of God I pray that you, too, will know how valuable you are to the King above all kings.

Pondering

I hear the waves crashing onto the shore.
I can see the sun rays shining through the clouds.
Is there anything that sounds more beautiful than the sights and sounds of the water as it hits the sand?
As I sit by the water, I ponder what my life will be like in the future.
I wonder what places I will go, or who I will meet on my journey.
I don't know what the future holds, but I know who holds the future.
So, as I sit and think, I know all is going to be okay.
I don't have to know everything or have it all together.
I just need to take one day at a time.
After all, what is there to worry about.
Life is good when I know where I'm going.

Give God Everything

I give you my fears, my hopes, and my dreams, I lay them at Your feet.
I give you my joys, my life, and my heart, I lay them at Your feet.
I give you my wants, plans, and desires, I lay them at Your feet.
I give you my tears, my good days, and my bad days, I lay them at Your feet.
I give you my family, friends, and my callings, I lay them at Your feet.
I give you my hands, feet, and mouth, I lay them at Your feet.
I give you my rights, my mind, and my emotions, I lay them at Your feet
I give you my feelings, my burdens, and my issues. I lay them at Your feet.
I give you my failure, my problems, and my needs, I lay them at Your feet.
I give you my money, my time, and my talents, I lay them at Your feet.
I give you my thoughts, my ways, and myself, I lay them at Your feet.
You can have all of me Lord.

Freed by His touch

Just one touch from you, that is all it takes for me to be whole.
Just one word is all it takes for me to be free.
Just one look, and I know life will never be the same.
This is what Jesus does, He takes my life and makes something wonderful out of it.
All I have to do is give Him my heart, and let Him make me into the person He wants me to be.
So, will I let Him make me whole?
Will I give Him the driver's seat, and let Him lead?
All He wants is my yes!
I love that God takes my imperfect life and uses it to reach others' lives.
So, I asked God to take my life and make it a vessel to be used by Him for His glory.

My Portion

You are the one that fills me up each day.
You are the one I run to.
Only You can satisfy me.
Nothing else will do.
I can fill Your arms around me as I sit in Your lap.
I know this is a safe place to be.
Just me and You right at this moment, nothing else matters.
All my cares and worries just seem to vanish when I am in Your presence.
I can hear Your heartbeat as I lean on Your chest, and I know it's all going to be okay.

Way Maker

God is the one who makes a way where there is no way!
He shines His light so you can see the path!
The road may be narrow, but with the help of God you can stay
on that path.
He brings the fire to purify your life.
He has hands of healing, a heart to touch the hardest of hearts.
His love is reaching all corners of the world!
He binds the wounds and sets the captives free.
The truth will set you free!
Will you follow the **Way Maker**?
He has a pathway for your life.
All He wants is your **yes** to Him.

My Psalm to Jesus

You are my song.
I sing my praise to you all day long.
You make me thankful for all I have.
You protect me from all harm.
When my enemies rise against me You protect me time and time again.
Keep me from complaining, and help me to be grateful in everything.
You are awesome far above all gods.
I pray I serve you all the days of my life.
You are the best thing that has ever happened to me.
I love You Lord.
Your laws are true and just.
Keep me in the way everlasting.
May I love others and see them the way you see them.
Keep my mouth from gossiping.
May my words bring life to others.
Yes, Lord You make me sore on wings like eagles.
You keep my feet from stumbling.
You're my hope, joy, and life.
All praise to You the King of Glory.

Someday

Someday when I meet you, I will know you are the one God has for me.
Together we will walk hand and hand down the isle knowing our love is forever.
I know it takes work to stay together, and serve one another in love.
With Jesus as the center I know we can accomplish so much for His kingdom.
Even though we may have difficult days, I believe this will make our love grow stronger.
I want to love you with all I am.
I can't wait to meet our kids if we ever have kids someday!
You are my best friend, the one who I can confide in, and pray with about anything and everything.
You are the one who makes my heart beat faster.
Your smile is what I look forward to seeing each day when I wake up.
I want to do life with you till death do us part.

Better Together

At 25 & 23, side by side, we said, "I do."
Couldn't imagine life without you.
Talks & walks; Cards & notes; Laughter & tears; Devotions &
prayers.
Side by side, Better together.
Life is seeming more complete.
3 awesome kids; 2 special spouses, too; 2 lovely grandkid: Of
course, being "Papa" and "Grandma" is very, very, sweet.
At 63 and 65, side by side, we'll say, "I do."
Couldn't imagine life without you.
Blessed fully by God, Rich with life and love.
So many reasons, looking forward to more
seasons.
Now, after 40 years, we know what we've known all along.
Side by side, We are better together!

Camp Jackson

You will always hold a special place in my heart.
The first year I worked up there I had no idea what I was getting into in my early 20's.
I needed a job and they needed a cook.
After the first spring and summer laboring there I was not certain I would back next summer, but the next year I filled out the application again to work in the kitchen once more.
One-year lead to the next and I worked on and off for 7 summers.
Some of the lessons I learned while working there are as follows:
If you say 1 negative thing about yourself or someone else, stop and say 3 nice things to yourself or to someone else!
Suck it up or in other words don't complain!
Treat others the way you want to be treated. AKA the golden rule!
Don't liter and leave each place you go to better then you found it!
Make receiving seconds of food, fun!
Teach kids how to cook/bake!
Make time for kids and invest in their lives!
Have fun!
There is a song for every occasion!
Learn CPR and First Aid after all you may save a life!
The 4-core values respect, responsibility, caring, and honesty are values to live by!
I still have some of the nametags I have made and the bear claw I was given one staff training week.
They serve as a reminder of all the special places Camp Jackson will have in my heart, and to uphold the 4-core values.
As I sit at Indian Circle writing this pome, I'm remined of all the special memories at the camp: going on pack out and getting caught in the rain!
The bear stakes!
Eating cold hobo stew!
Hiking the mountains trails, and going to outpost at night!
Cooking for 150ish staff and campers!

Campfires, Words of Wisdom, and s'mores!
Flag raising/lowering!
Nightly activities Capture the Mattress (CTM) was my favorite
game and the Thursday night dance was a blast!
Shooting guns, riding horses, canoeing, camping, arts, high
ropes, archery, team building, and mail call at lunches, so many
memories I will treasure for life.
Because of Camp Jackson I went to culinary school, and studied
nutrition and ended up doing my internship there.
Now, I have cooked all over the world and know this is my
passion.
So thanks Camp Jackson for all the memories, laughs, lessons,
and love I have felt there.

Rushing Water

As I sit in the Rye Park, I can hear the rushing water rushing in the creek nearby.
The mountain run off is filling the creeks with a loud roar of water.
I'm looking forward to a summer without drought, no forest fires, or firer bans.
Is there a any sweeter sound then the sound of rushing water?
I miss my days at Camp Jackson and falling a sleep to the sound of rushing water as I slept with my cabin
windows open.
Makes me wish I could fall asleep to the sound of rushing water each night.

Peaches and Cream

Oh, the joy that shows on the face when a person eats a peach.
The juice from the peach runs down the arm and on the ground.
I can see the faces light up when they see the tents come up, and realize the peaches are in season.
There is nothing quite like a peach when it comes to juicy fruit.
The Palisade peaches are simply the best kind of peaches.
I have not found a peach to compare.
Oh Henry, how I miss you come December.
In March when I wish I could have a peach pie I realize just how short the peach season is.

www.ingramcontent.com/pod-product-compliance
Lightning Source LLC
Chambersburg PA
CBHW031555310726
48973CB00003B/832